For Finbar
and Jock

First published 1994 by Walker Books Ltd
87 Vauxhall Walk, London SE11 5HJ

10 9 8 7 6 5 4 3 2 1

© 1994 Flora McDonnell

This book is set in New Baskerville.

Printed in Belgium

British Library Cataloguing
in Publication Data
A catalogue record for this book is
available from the British Library.

ISBN 0-7445-2246-3

I LOVe Animals

Flora McDonnell

WALKER BOOKS
LONDON

I love Jock,
my dog.

I love
the ducks

waddling to
the water.

I love the hens
hopping up
and down.

I love the goat

racing across
the field.

I love the donkey

braying
"hee-haw!"

I love the cow
swishing her tail.

I love the pig with

all her little piglets.

I love the pony

rolling

over

and

over.

I love the sheep
bleating to
her lamb.

I love

the cat

washing her
kittens.

I love the turkey

strutting
round
the yard.

I love all
the animals.

I hope they love me.